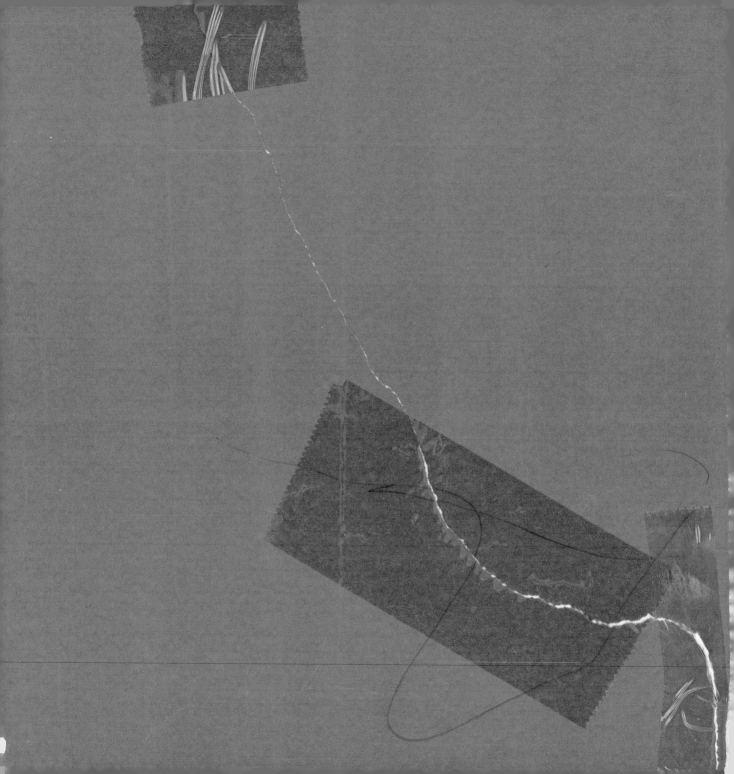

THE SUNSHINE SQUAD

Discovering What Makes YOU Special

Jamie Michalak • *Illustrated by* **Lorian Tu**

i≈i Charlesbridge

At 123 Sunshine Street,
everyone is welcome and
there's a story behind each door.

Today a story even begins on one.

This is Oliver, also known as the Masked Artist.

mask

trail mix
(for a boost
of energy
when saving
the world)

comic

colored
pencils

pencil
of
power

favorite
cape

tights
peeking out
of jeans
(you never
know when
you might
need them!)

(He's a little into superheroes—and loves drawing comics.)

The only thing Oliver loves more than making comics is hanging out with his best friends:

Everyone reads Oliver's sign on the front door.

Not only do they go to school together, they also
all live in the same building—like one big family.

Curious, the kids get ready
to meet up with their friends.

Mia grabs her favorite skateboard.

"Let's go,
Fuzzypants!
Are you squealing
because you're
happy?"

"I'm
ready
to roll!"

Sophie chooses
one of her many
pets to bring along.

"Whoopee cushion
or rubber rat?"

Lucas scans his
shelves of joke supplies.
He picks out a prank
to pull on his friends.

Lucas heads downstairs. And Tommy, his little brother, tags along.

"What's your super idea, Oliver?" Mia asks.

"I'm reading about a league of superheroes," Oliver explains, "and I want to start our own! We can use this spot as headquarters, and wear capes, and—"

"Wait," says Lucas.
"There's just one problem."

"What's that?" Oliver asks.

"We don't have superpowers!" Lucas cries.

"We'll pretend," says Oliver.
"Our talents can be our superpowers."

"If I had a superpower," Oliver says, "it would be making things come to life with my pencil. If a monster ever attacks our street, I'll draw a trap. *POW!*"

"Oh, I get it," Mia says.
"With my skateboard,
I'd spin into a tornado and
blow the monster away.
BAM! So long, stinky!"

"I'm a master of surprise," says Lucas. "Would a monster ever see **THIS** coming? I think not."

"I'd teach the monster to be nice and make it my pet," says Sophie. "I'd learn everything about it. I wonder if it would fit in my room."

"Then we'd save our neighborhood!" says Oliver.
"You need a superpower, too, Tommy. Or you
can't be in our league. What's your talent?"

But nobody knows. Not even Tommy.

"Hmm." Oliver thinks.
"You must be good at something."

"He's good at tagging along," Lucas offers.

"It's okay, Tommy," says Mia.
"You'll be super like us when you're older."

"You're just little," says Sophie.
"Like my kitten, Fluffy."

Tommy makes a face.
"But I don't want to be Fluffy."

"Fluffy isn't the best name for
a superhero," Lucas agrees.

Too little. Too young.
Always following the others—
a tagalong.

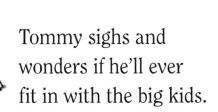

Tommy sighs and
wonders if he'll ever
fit in with the big kids.

Without him, the others practice their superpowers.
Meanwhile Mrs. Felix struggles to open the door.

"I'll help," says Tommy.

"Thank you," she replies. "You're always spreading sunshine."

Just then an orange rolls out of her bag
and down the steps . . .

Whoosh! goes Mia's skateboard.

"Squeak!" goes Fuzzypants.

"Cool!" says Mia.
"I never knew guinea pigs could skateboard."

"FUZZYPANTS!" shouts Sophie.
"Somebody save him!"

They try.

Screeech!

"Tommy, you saved Fuzzypants!" Sophie exclaims.

"And the day!"
says Oliver.

"And the orange,"
says Lucas.

"But I still don't have a superpower," says Tommy.

"I think you just found it," says Oliver.

"I did?" Tommy asks.

"You're a helper, little dude," says Mia.
"Kindness is your superpower."

"While we were pretending to be superheroes," Sophie says, "you were the real hero."

"Tommy, you gave me a new idea!" Oliver exclaims. "Instead of pretending to be superheroes, we'll be a league of everyday heroes who help our neighbors."

"Yes!" Mia cheers. "We can spread sunshine in so many ways."

"We can tell jokes," says Lucas.

"And draw cards for people," says Oliver.

"And walk our neighbors' dogs," Sophie adds.

"And give out lemonade on a hot day," Tommy suggests.

"Now all we need is a name," Mia says.

Oliver smiles. "Leave that to me."

At 123 Sunshine Street, everyone is welcome and there's a story behind each door.

Today a story even ends on one.

The Sunshine Squad

By: Oliver

To super T, a real hero!
from the Masked Artist

You Do It Your Way, and I'll Do It Mine

The hardest part about being the youngest in the family is not that you're shorter than everyone else. It's not that you can't keep up. It's not that you're the last to get a serving of snacks.

All that is nowhere near as bad being told, "No, do it this way." If I asked to help Grandma when she was baking her famous cornbread, she'd slide the big mixing bowl to where I could reach it. I'd stir the batter, but Grandma would stop me and say, "No, do it this way." She showed me how she wanted it stirred, and I did my best to imitate her.

If I asked Dad how I could help when he was working in the garage, he'd hand me a wrench. I could get about two cranks on a bolt in before he'd stop me and say, "No, do it this way, or you'll strip the bolt." I did my best not to blunt the corners.

When my older sister Missy and I dressed up our dolls, I was put in charge of doing the dolls' hair. Three wraps into a lovely braid, my sister would reach for the doll and say, "No, do it this way." She would twist the hair and pin it, and I'd try hard to do it that way.

I knew they were all trying to teach me how to do something faster or better. But I didn't like feeling wrong all the time.

One weekend, my family got together to help Grandma and Grandpa with gardening.

My cousin Brian, the oldest, got to work mowing the lawn. His sister Jaime and my sister Missy got to plant all the flowers in the garden. The adults started cutting a stone-paved walkway around the garden.

I asked what I could do. Grandpa led me to the big juniper bush at the front of the lawn. Long, frizzy branches grew out in all directions. The bush looked like a big, green porcupine. Grandpa used a pair of long-handled gardening shears to chomp off the bristles.

Clip! Clip! Clip! Grandpa flattened out one side of the juniper. He gave me the shears and told me to trim the other side. He waited to watch, but I didn't do anything.

"I can do it by myself, Grandpa," I said.

Grandpa tipped his hat with a wink and said he would come back. When he was gone, I lifted the big heavy shears and clipped at the jagged bristles.

I missed.

I clipped again. This time a big wad of green bits crunched between the blades. But they jammed the blades together. I pulled and tugged and finally freed the shears. I couldn't trim the juniper the right way. I leaned the big shears against the fence and ran into the house. I took a pair of regular scissors and ran back out to the bush.

Snip. Snip. Snip.

Little bristles fell to the ground.

I took a step back to inspect my work. The porcupine pincushion looked neat on my side.

Grandpa watched me with the scissors and said, "That way will take all day."

I knew he was about to tell me: "No, do it this way." But he stopped. After a minute, he lifted his cap, scratched his head, and laughed. "Your side looks better than mine."

I gawked. "You mean my way isn't wrong?"

"No, ma'am." Grandpa leveled the big shears at the juniper bush and said, "You do it your way, and I'll do it mine."

Grandpa cut the really big and bristly branches, and then I trimmed up all the pokey, prickly bits. We squared off all four sides in no time. I showed Grandpa my trimming techniques. For the most part, he did exactly what I showed him. His way might have been a little different, but it got the job done.

As I grew up I still learned from other people when they showed me new methods, but I realized the point is not always to imitate. Being different is fine, which is why I figure out my own way of doing things.

Adapted from the story by Jenny Mason, *Chicken Soup for the Soul: Think Positive for Kids*. © 2013 Chicken Soup for the Soul, LLC. All rights reserved.

10 Things You Can Do to Spread Sunshine

(You might need a parent or caregiver's permission or help.)

1. Donate toys you no longer play with to someone who might like them.
2. Bake cookies for a neighbor.
3. Make a thank-you card for your teacher.
4. Do your chores without being asked.
5. Read a story to someone.
6. Pick up trash around the neighborhood.
7. Write happy messages on the sidewalk with chalk.
8. Donate your old clothes to a charity.
9. Make a bird feeder.
10. Call or visit an elderly relative. They will love to hear your stories or get a piece of your artwork.

How else can YOU spread some sunshine?

For my own little Sunshine Squad: Siena, Jack, and Mila—J. M.

For my personal Sunshine Squad:
Mr. Floyd Cooper, Las Musas, Molly, Sam, and Ollie.
Thank you for shining on me always.—L. T.

Published by Charlesbridge
9 Galen Street
Watertown, MA 02472
(617) 926-0329
www.charlesbridge.com

Library of Congress Cataloging-in-Publication Data
Names: Michalak, Jamie, author. | Tu, Lorian, illustrator.
Title: Chicken soup for the soul kids: the Sunshine Squad: discovering what makes you special /Jamie Michalak;
    illustrated by Lorian Tu.
Description: Watertown, MA: Charlesbridge, [2021] | Series: Chicken soup for the soul kids |
Audience: Ages 4–7. | Audience: Grades K–1. |
Summary: Best friends Oliver, Sophie, Mia, Lucas, and Lucas's little brother, Tommy, all live at 123 Sunshine
    Street, and Oliver (who loves and draws comics) wants them to form a league of superheroes—but first they
    have to figure out just what superpowers they can claim.
Identifiers: LCCN 2020055575 (print) | LCCN 2020055576 (ebook) | ISBN 9781623542740 (hardcover) |
    ISBN 9781632898920 (ebook)
Subjects: LCSH: Superheroes—Juvenile fiction. | Best friends—Juvenile fiction. | Kindness—Juvenile fiction. |
    Conduct of life—Juvenile fiction. | CYAC: Superheroes—Fiction. | Best friends—Fiction. | Friendship—
    Fiction. | Kindness—Fiction. | Conduct of life—Fiction.
Classification: LCC PZ7.W58453 Su 2021 (print) | LCC PZ7.W58453 (ebook) | DDC [E]—dc23
LC record available at https://lccn.loc.gov/2020055575
LC ebook record available at https://lccn.loc.gov/2020055576

Printed in China
(hc) 10 9 8 7 6 5 4 3 2 1

Illustrations created digitally
Display type set in Midnight Chalker by Hanoded
Text type set in Oxford by Roger White
Color separations and printing by 1010 Printing International Limited in Huizhou, Guangdong, China
Production supervision by Jennifer Most Delaney
Designed by Kristen Nobles